Dear Parent:

Your child's love of reading starts here!

Every child learns to read in a different way and at his or her own speed. Some go back and forth between reading levels and read favorite books again and again. Others read through each level in order. You can help your young reader improve and become more confident by encouraging his or her own interests and abilities. From books your child reads with you to the first books he or she reads alone, there are I Can Read Books for every stage of reading:

SHARED READING
Basic language, word repetition, and whimsical illustrations, ideal for sharing with your emergent reader

BEGINNING READING
Short sentences, familiar words, and simple concepts for children eager to read on their own

READING WITH HELP
Engaging stories, longer sentences, and language play for developing readers

READING ALONE
Complex plots, challenging vocabulary, and high-interest topics for the independent reader

I Can Read Books have introduced children to the joy of reading since 1957. Featuring award-winning authors and illustrators and a fabulous cast of beloved characters, I Can Read Books set the standard for beginning readers.

A lifetime of discovery begins with the magical words "I Can Read!"

Visit www.icanread.com for information
on enriching your child's reading experience.

To my children, fighting
evil creatures inside me
so fearlessly
—A.Z.

I Can Read® and I Can Read Book® are trademarks of HarperCollins Publishers.

Copyright © 2019 DC Comics
SHAZAM! and all related characters and elements © & ™ DC Comics and Warner Bros. Entertainment Inc.
(S19)

HARP41773

Library of Congress Control Number: 2018961829
ISBN 978-0-06-289863-0

Book design by Erica De Chavez
19 20 21 22 23 LSCC 10 9 8 7 6 5 4 3 2 1 ❖ First Edition

I Can Read!

3
READING ALONE

SHAZAM!

A SHAZAM SHOWDOWN

Adapted by Alexandra West
Illustrated by Aleksandar Zolotic

Shazam! created by
C.C. Beck and Bill Parker

HARPER
An Imprint of HarperCollinsPublishers

Shazam is a Super Hero.

But he is not an ordinary Super Hero.

Shazam is also a kid named Billy Batson.

He was given super powers by a Wizard.

His powers made him a Champion.

They also made him famous.

Shazam liked being famous.

Shazam's best friend, Freddy,

thought that Shazam was getting a big head.

But Shazam's fans wanted him
to show off his powers.
"Shazam! Shazam!" they chanted.
So Shazam sent lightning into the sky.
But the lightning hit a bus on the bridge!

"Look what you did!" Freddy shouted.

"That bus is full of people!"

Shazam was in shock.

He had to help!

He rushed off to the rescue.

Suddenly, the bus began to fall off the bridge!

WHAM!

Using his super-strength,

Shazam caught the bus in his arms!

He made it just in time.

Everyone cheered for their hero, Shazam!

Meanwhile, the evil villain Dr. Sivana
was looking for Shazam.

Dr. Sivana had been secretly tracking him.

He wanted Shazam's powers for himself.
And he was ready to take them by force.

Long ago, Dr. Sivana had also met the Wizard.

The Wizard said he could never be a Champion.

That made Dr. Sivana very angry.

He spent his whole life trying to find the Wizard.

When he found the Wizard, Dr. Sivana freed

seven evil creatures that had been trapped.

They became a part of Dr. Sivana.

They made him powerful.

But Dr. Sivana wanted to be a Champion.

And to be a Champion, he needed Shazam's powers.

Now was Dr. Sivana's moment to steal
Shazam's powers and become a Champion.
But when Dr. Sivana confronted Shazam,
Shazam thought he was just another fan.
"Listen, no pictures please," Shazam said.

Suddenly, Dr. Sivana threw a powerful punch,
but Shazam quickly blocked his fist.
Dr. Sivana launched into an epic attack,
and Shazam was forced to fight back.

Dr. Sivana grabbed Shazam by the collar
and began to squeeze.

Dr. Sivana shot into the sky,

taking Shazam high above the clouds.

"Let me go!" Shazam cried.

So the villain let Shazam go.

Shazam began to fall quickly back to Earth.

"Fly!" Shazam said to himself.

"Come on, I know I can do it!"

Shazam fell, but he did not hit the ground.

His positive thinking had worked!

Before Shazam could catch his breath,

Dr. Sivana found him again.

He threw Shazam into the ground.

Freddy looked on in shock.

"What's going on?" Freddy called out.

"And who's the evil guy?"

Suddenly, Dr. Sivana and Shazam
exploded through the floor of a mall!

The battle continued as Dr. Sivana
smashed Shazam through a ceiling.
Thinking quickly, Shazam hid.
He began to talk to himself in the mirror.
"You don't have to fight this guy," he said.
"You can just run."

BOOM!

Dr. Sivana tackled Shazam.

The villain sent him flying

through a toy store.

Shazam crashed through the toy shelves.

Dr. Sivana charged at Shazam.

The villain sprinted across a floor piano,
making music as he ran.

Dr. Sivana grabbed Shazam.

"I am the rightful Champion," he said.

"Your powers are mine!"

CRASH!

Dr. Sivana threw Shazam
through the store window.
Shazam hit the ground hard.
He cried out in pain.

Shazam lay on the ground.

He was defeated.

Then Shazam realized that Dr. Sivana
wouldn't recognize him as Billy Batson.

"SHAZAM!" he said.

Lightning broke the glass ceiling above him.

Shazam was a kid again.

He was Billy Batson.

"Billy!" Freddy shouted through the chaos.
"I can't believe you fought a real super-villain!
I think he wants your powers."
The two friends quickly walked through
the mall doors and headed for home.
Billy smiled. "I think you're right.
But next time we see him, we'll be ready."

Turn the page for more on
this moment from the film!

RISE TO FAME

Freddy thinks Shazam's fame is going to his head. Shazam shows off his powers for the crowd.

NICE CATCH!

When Shazam's lightning strike accidentally hits a bus, it's up to the new hero to save the passengers inside.

MEET THE EVIL DR. SIVANA

After secretly tracking Shazam, Dr. Sivana has come to take the hero's powers for himself.

A MEGA MALL MELTDOWN!

"WHO'S THE EVIL GUY?"

It's Shazam versus Dr. Sivana in a head-to-head battle! A confused Freddy looks on as Dr. Sivana drives Shazam into the ground and up into a mall.

PIANO PANDEMONIUM

When Shazam and Dr. Sivana find themselves in a toy store, they make music with their feet across a floor piano.

FACING A SUPER-VILLAIN

Dr. Sivana throws Shazam through the toy store window. Shazam decides to transform back into Billy and slip away unnoticed.

BILLY MAKES A PLAN

With the knowledge that an evil super-villain is after him, Billy makes plans to take down the villain and defend his city.